MAY 1 5 2007

P9-DMW-733

Raves for *A Confederacy of Dunces*

"A gem—one of the funniest books ever written."
—*New Republic*

"There is a touch of genius about Toole and what he has created."
—*Publishers Weekly*

"As hilarious as it indisputably is, *A Confederacy of Dunces* is a serious important work."
—*Los Angeles Herald Examiner*

"If a book's price is measured against the laughs it provokes, *A Confederacy of Dunces* is the bargain of the year."
—*Time*

"The mix of high and low comedy is almost stroboscopic: brilliant, relentless, delicious, perhaps even classic."
—*Kirkus Reviews*

"A brilliant and evocative novel."
—*San Francisco Chronicle*

"I found myself laughing out loud again and again as I read this ribald book."
—*Christian Science Monitor*

"The episodes explode one after the other like fireworks on a stormy night. No doubt about it, this book is destined to become a classic."
—*The Baltimore Sun*

"An astonishingly original and assured comic spree."
—*New York*

"The dialogue is superbly mad. You simply sweep along, unbelievably entranced."
—*The Boston Globe*

A Confederacy of Dunces

When a true genius appears in the world,
you may know him by this sign, that the dunces
are all in confederacy against him.

Jonathan Swift—
"THOUGHTS ON VARIOUS SUBJECTS,
MORAL AND DIVERTING"

one might not be bad enough, or might be just good enough, so that I would have to keep reading.

In this case I read on. And on. First with the sinking feeling that it was not bad enough to quit, then with a prickle of interest, then a growing excitement, and finally an incredulity: surely it was not possible that it was so good. I shall resist the temptation to say what first made me gape, grin, laugh out loud, shake my head in wonderment. Better let the reader make the discovery on his own.

Here at any rate is Ignatius Reilly, without progenitor in any literature I know of—slob extraordinary, a mad Oliver Hardy, a fat Don Quixote, a perverse Thomas Aquinas rolled into one—who is in violent revolt against the entire modern age, lying in his flannel nightshirt, in a back bedroom on Constantinople Street in New Orleans, who between gigantic seizures of flatulence and eructations is filling dozens of Big Chief tablets with invective.

His mother thinks he needs to go to work. He does, in a succession of jobs. Each job rapidly escalates into a lunatic adventure, a full-blown disaster; yet each has, like Don Quixote's, its own eerie logic.

His girlfriend, Myrna Minkoff of the Bronx, thinks he needs sex. What happens between Myrna and Ignatius is like no other boy-meets-girl story in my experience.

By no means a lesser virtue of Toole's novel is his rendering of the particularities of New Orleans, its back streets, its out-of-the-way neighborhoods, its odd speech, its ethnic whites—and one black in whom Toole has achieved the near-impossible, a superb comic character of immense wit and resourcefulness without the least trace of Rastus minstrelsy.

A
Confederacy
of DUNCES

JOHN KENNEDY TOOLE

Foreword by Walker Percy

WINGS BOOKS

New York ▲ Avenel, New Jersey

DISCARDED
BRADFORD WG
PUBLIC LIBRARY

BRADFORD WG LIBRARY
100 HOLLAND COURT, BOX 130
BRADFORD, ONT. L3Z 2A7

Copyright © 1980 by Thelma D. Toole

All rights reserved under International and Pan–American
Copyright Conventions.

No part of this book may be reproduced or transmitted in any form
or by any means electronic or mechanical including photocopying,
recording, or by any information storage and retrieval system, without
permission in writing from the publisher.

This 1996 edition is published by Wings Books,
a division of Random House Value Publishing, Inc.,
40 Engelhard Avenue, Avenel, New Jersey 07001,
by arrangement with Louisiana State University Press.

Wings Books and colophon are trademarks of
Random House Value Publishing, Inc.

Random House
New York • Toronto • London • Sydney • Auckland
http://www.randomhouse.com/

Book design by Kathryn W. Plosica

Printed and bound in the United States of America

Library of Congress Cataloging-in Publication Data

Toole, John Kennedy, 1937—1969.
    A confederacy of dunces / John Kennedy Toole ; foreword by
Walker Percy.
        p.   cm.
    ISBN 0-517-12270-7
    I. Title.
PS3570.O54C66   1994
813'.54—dc20   94-30317
                                                CIP

15 14 13 12 11 10

FOREWORD

PERHAPS THE BEST WAY to introduce this novel—which
on my third reading of it astounds me even more than
the first—is to tell of my first encounter with it. While I
was teaching at Loyola in 1976 I began to get telephone
calls from a lady unknown to me. What she proposed
was preposterous. It was not that she had written a
couple of chapters of a novel and wanted to get into my
class. It was that her son, who was dead, had written an
entire novel during the early sixties, a big novel, and she
wanted me to read it. Why would I want to do that? I
asked her. Because it is a great novel, she said.

Over the years I have become very good at getting
out of things I don't want to do. And if ever there was
something I didn't want to do, this was surely it: to deal
with the mother of a dead novelist and, worst of all, to
have to read a manuscript that she said was *great*, and
that, as it turned out, was a badly smeared, scarcely
readable carbon.

But the lady was persistent, and it somehow came
to pass that she stood in my office handing me the hefty
manuscript. There was no getting out of it; only one
hope remained—that I could read a few pages and that
they would be bad enough for me, in good conscience,
to read no farther. Usually I can do just that. Indeed the
first paragraph often suffices. My only fear was that this

vii

A
Confederacy
of DUNCES

JOHN KENNEDY TOOLE

Foreword by Walker Percy

WINGS BOOKS

DISCARDED
BRADFORD WG
PUBLIC LIBRARY

New York ▲ Avenel, New Jersey

BRADFORD WG LIBRARY
100 HOLLAND COURT, BOX 130
BRADFORD, ONT. L37 2A7

Copyright © 1980 by Thelma D. Toole

All rights reserved under International and Pan–American
Copyright Conventions.

No part of this book may be reproduced or transmitted in any form
or by any means electronic or mechanical including photocopying,
recording, or by any information storage and retrieval system, without
permission in writing from the publisher.

This 1996 edition is published by Wings Books,
a division of Random House Value Publishing, Inc.,
40 Engelhard Avenue, Avenel, New Jersey 07001,
by arrangement with Louisiana State University Press.

Wings Books and colophon are trademarks of
Random House Value Publishing, Inc.

Random House
New York • Toronto • London • Sydney • Auckland
http://www.randomhouse.com/

Book design by Kathryn W. Plosica

Printed and bound in the United States of America

Library of Congress Cataloging-in Publication Data

Toole, John Kennedy, 1937—1969.
    A confederacy of dunces / John Kennedy Toole ; foreword by
Walker Percy.
      p.   cm.
    ISBN 0-517-12270-7
    I. Title.
PS3570.054C66   1994
813'.54—dc20   94-30317
                                                CIP

15 14 13 12 11 10

FOREWORD

PERHAPS THE BEST WAY to introduce this novel—which on my third reading of it astounds me even more than the first—is to tell of my first encounter with it. While I was teaching at Loyola in 1976 I began to get telephone calls from a lady unknown to me. What she proposed was preposterous. It was not that she had written a couple of chapters of a novel and wanted to get into my class. It was that her son, who was dead, had written an entire novel during the early sixties, a big novel, and she wanted me to read it. Why would I want to do that? I asked her. Because it is a great novel, she said.

Over the years I have become very good at getting out of things I don't want to do. And if ever there was something I didn't want to do, this was surely it: to deal with the mother of a dead novelist and, worst of all, to have to read a manuscript that she said was *great*, and that, as it turned out, was a badly smeared, scarcely readable carbon.

But the lady was persistent, and it somehow came to pass that she stood in my office handing me the hefty manuscript. There was no getting out of it; only one hope remained—that I could read a few pages and that they would be bad enough for me, in good conscience, to read no farther. Usually I can do just that. Indeed the first paragraph often suffices. My only fear was that this one might not be bad enough, or might be just good enough, so that I would have to keep reading.

In this case I read on. And on. First with the sinking feeling that it was not bad enough to quit, then with a prickle of interest, then a growing excitement, and finally an incredulity: surely it was not possible that it was so good. I shall resist the temptation to say what first made me gape, grin, laugh out loud, shake my head in wonderment. Better let the reader make the discovery on his own.

Here at any rate is Ignatius Reilly, without progenitor in any literature I know of—slob extraordinary, a mad Oliver Hardy, a fat Don Quixote, a perverse Thomas Aquinas rolled into one—who is in violent revolt against the entire modern age, lying in his flannel nightshirt, in a back bedroom on Constantinople Street in New Orleans, who between gigantic seizures of flatulence and eructations is filling dozens of Big Chief tablets with invective.

His mother thinks he needs to go to work. He does, in a succession of jobs. Each job rapidly escalates into a lunatic adventure, a full-blown disaster; yet each has, like Don Quixote's, its own eerie logic.

His girlfriend, Myrna Minkoff of the Bronx, thinks he needs sex. What happens between Myrna and Ignatius is like no other boy-meets-girl story in my experience.

By no means a lesser virtue of Toole's novel is his rendering of the particularities of New Orleans, its back streets, its out-of-the-way neighborhoods, its odd speech, its ethnic whites—and one black in whom Toole has achieved the near-impossible, a superb comic character of immense wit and resourcefulness without the least trace of Rastus minstrelsy.